Published in 2021 by Groundwood Books / House of Anansi Press
groundwoodbooks.com

Groundwood Books respectfully acknowledges that the land on which
we operate is the Traditional Territory of many Nations, including the
Anishinabeg, the Wendat and the Haudenosaunee. It is also the Treaty Lands
of the Mississaugas of the Credit.

We gratefully acknowledge for their financial support of our publishing
program the Canada Council for the Arts, the Ontario Arts Council and the
Government of Canada.

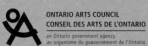

Library and Archives Canada Cataloguing in Publication
Title: Song for the snow / words by Jon-Erik Lappano ; pictures by Byron
Eggenschwiler.
Names: Lappano, Jon-Erik, author. | Eggenschwiler, Byron, illustrator.
Identifiers: Canadiana (print) 2020039424X | Canadiana (ebook)
20200394266 | ISBN 9781773062686 (hardcover) | ISBN 9781773062693
(EPUB) | ISBN 9781773065823 (Kindle)
Classification: LCC PS8623.A73745 S66 2021 | DDC jC813/.6—dc23

The illustrations were created digitally.
Design by Michael Solomon
Printed and bound in Canada

For our children, who call
for us to play in the snow.
JEL

For Vivian and Sofia.
BE

Song for the Snow

words by Jon-Erik Lappano

pictures by Byron Eggenschwiler

Groundwood Books
House of Anansi Press
Toronto / Berkeley

In early winter, Freya dreamed of the snow.

She had always loved the snow, how it
covered everything in softness and dusted
the trees like powdered sugar on her favorite
spice cakes.

Freya usually knew when the snow was coming. First, the air grew cold. Frost covered the grass and crunched under her feet. Her breath rose like smoke above her.

But the snow hadn't come to Freya's town
for a long time. For the past two winters, the air
hadn't changed. The grass stayed wet with dew,
and her breath remained invisible.

Freya's memories of the snow were
beginning to fade. She longed to see it again, to
run and jump in it and pack it in her hands.

One morning, she asked her mother,
"When will it snow again?"
"When it's cold," said her mother. Steam
rose in swirls from her cup of coffee.

Freya looked at her father.

"When will it be cold?"

"Someday," he said, crunching into his toast. The sound reminded Freya of her boots on the frozen ground.

Maybe the snow is lost, she thought.

Freya went to the market with her father. She gazed at the cakes and imagined walking over their snowy tops, sinking her feet into the sugar, sledding down their frosted sides and skating over the glass plates.

Just then, above the noise of the busy market, a soft, twinkling melody danced in Freya's ears.

Drawn toward the tune, she came to a table of trinkets. Behind it, a woman was holding a beautiful snow globe.

"This song is very old and special," the woman said, as she shook the globe and wound its silver key. "Every winter for generations, our townspeople would sing it. Some say it was the magic of the song that called the snow home."

Freya stared with wonder as swirling,
sparkling flakes drifted down onto the
tiny village.

"A gift," the woman said, passing the
globe to Freya.

On the way home, Freya held her new treasure
close, playing the melody again and again.

At bedtime, she played it for her mother.

"I know this song," her mother said, closing her eyes. "My grandmother sang it on nights when the snow was so deep it felt like we'd disappear beneath it."

"*Come home, snow,*" she sang. "*Fall from high … cover the trees and fill the sky …*"

The next morning, Freya woke early. She took the globe and went out into the dark winter morning.

Freya shook the globe and wound its silver key. She closed her eyes and sang the words her mother had sung the night before.

"Come home, snow," she whispered.

But the snow didn't come.

The next morning, Freya tried again.

And the next morning,

and the next.

But still, the snow didn't come.

On the radio, Freya heard someone say that the snow wouldn't come this year, and that it might be gone for good.

She stared out at the flat, gray sky. Maybe the snow was too far away to hear her song. Maybe she wasn't singing loud enough.

From the radio, the full, rich sound of a choir sang out.

That night, Freya dreamed of a great flock of birds. They flew up past the trees and over the valley, carried by the wind, landing on faraway, snow-covered mountains.

The next day, she carried the snow globe to school. She told her friends about the song's magic and sang the words as the melody played.

Soon other children were singing the song at home.
As they sang, distant memories of cozy, snow-filled
nights returned to their parents. They hummed the
familiar tune as they went about their days.

Slowly, the words came back to everyone in Freya's town. The song once again filled their homes and hearts.

And then early one morning, before the stars
faded, the wind changed.

Freya went outside and breathed in deep.
The air was cold. Frost crunched under her feet.
Her breath rose like smoke to the sky.
As she began to sing, a single, lonely
snowflake drifted into town.

And then another.

And another, and another, until the sky was completely filled with snow. The snow dusted the branches of trees sugar-white, and the town disappeared beneath it.

Snowflakes fell on Freya's hair. They settled on her eyelashes. They tickled her nose and brushed against her cheeks, as she sang out her song to the snow.